8/02
E
SWE

WE CAN READ!™

Just Call Me J. P.

by Jacqueline Sweeney

photography by G. K. & Vikki Hart
photo illustration by Blind Mice Studio

BENCHMARK BOOKS

MARSHALL CAVENDISH
NEW YORK

For the Griffin Bunnyheads:
Tyler Alonzo and Alex Mateo

With thanks to Daria Murphy, Reading Specialist,
K-8 English Language Arts Coordinator,
for reading this manuscript with care and for writing
the "We Can Read and Learn" activity guide.

Benchmark Books
Marshall Cavendish Corporation
99 White Plains Road
Tarrytown, New York 10591

Text copyright © 2000 by Jacqueline Sweeney
Photo illustrations copyright © 2000 by G. K. & Vikki Hart
and Mark & Kendra Empey

Library of Congress Cataloging-in-Publication Data
Sweeney, Jacqueline.
Just call me J. P. / Jacqueline Sweeney.
p. cm. — (We can read!)
Summary: James Philip Bunny is always squinting and he is unhappy about being
mistaken for his twin brother, until his parents find a way to solve his two prob-
lems at one time.
ISBN 0-7614-0922-X (lib. bdg.)
[1. Rabbits—Fiction. 2. Twins—Fiction. 3. Eyeglasses—Fiction.]
I. Title. II. Series: We can read! (New York, N.Y.)
PZ7.S974255Ju 1999 [E]—dc21 98-43344 CIP
AC

Printed in Italy

3 5 6 4 2

Characters

Papa

 Mama

Jim (J.P.)

 Tim

Mimsy

 Ruby

Bud

 Eddie

Ron

Hildy

Molly

Gus

One, two, three, four …
Papa counted bunny heads.

"Tim, Mimsy, Ruby, Bud —
where's Jim?"

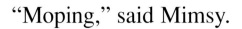

"Moping," said Mimsy.

"Ron the Toad called him Tim."

"Not again!" said Mama.

"Oh, it's hard to be a twin."

"I see him," said Papa.

Jim was hopping down Pebble Path.

"Why is he squinting?" asked Mimsy.

"I don't know," Papa said.

THUMP!

Jim tripped on a branch.

He rolled into Briar Hollow.

"Eddie called me Timmy," he cried.

"Ron called me Tim!"

Jimmy stomped his foot.

"I don't want to be a twin!" he shouted.

"I'm James Philip Bunny!

I'm ME!"

"We could call you J.P.!"  cried Mimsy.

"J.P.!" squealed Ruby.

"J.P.!" squeaked Baby Bud.

Jim shook his head.

"I'll still LOOK like Tim."

"You could paint yourself blue," said Ruby.

"Pull back your ears and
wear a red hat," said Tim.

"Bark like a dog."

"Meow like a cat," said Mimsy.

That night Jim dreamed he
was looking into Willow Pond.

Tim was looking too.

But who was who?

Papa and Jim got up early.

"Where did they go?" asked Mimsy.

"I can't tell you," said Mama.

"It's a surprise."

They waited and waited…

Ruby counted briar thorns.

Mimsy counted weeds.

Bud counted ladybugs.

Tim counted seeds.

Finally, Mama counted bunny heads.

*T*hump, *thumpity,*
thumpity, thump...

In hopped Papa and Jim.

"Look!" squealed Ruby.

"Glasses!" said Tim.

"Jim's different," said Mimsy.

"He doesn't squint."

"Do they hurt your nose?" asked Ruby.

"Do they make you feel funny?" asked Tim.

"No!" said Jim, "I feel like ME!

Like James Philip Bunny.

Just call me J. P."

WE CAN READ AND LEARN

The following activities are designed to enhance literacy development. *Just Call Me J. P.* can help children to build skills in vocabulary, phonics, and creative writing; to explore self-awareness; and to make connections between literature and other subject areas such as science and math.

J. P.'S CHALLENGE WORDS

Discuss the meanings of these words and use them in sentences:

branch	briar	count	dream
hollow	mope	pebble	shout
squeak	squeal	squint	stomp
surprise	thorn	twin	willow

FUN WITH PHONICS

Bunny Bingo reinforces listening and phonics skills. To make bingo cards, draw nine boxes on several sheets of paper. In each box, write short i words from the list below. Each card should have words in different boxes so that no two cards are the same.

Short i words:

Jim/Jimmy
Tim/Timmy
Mimsy
Philip
him
tripped
twin
still
willow
did
squint
different

Tim	squint	Jim
still		did
willow	twin	tripped

To play bunny bingo, a teacher or parent reads the story while children listen for short i words. Each time a word on the card is heard, they cover it with a coin, chip, or cotton ball bunny tail. The first player to cover a row across, down, or diagonally wins the game.

30

J. P.'s New Adventure. Cut out pictures from old magazines that identify short i words. Use them along with short i words or rhyming words from this story to write a new adventure about J. P. and his glasses.

Rhyming words:

Tim • Jim • him   seeds • weeds   he • me • be
see • three • J. P.   shook • look   Timmy • Jimmy
too • who

CREATIVE WRITING

Acrostic Antics. J. P. Bunny was a special little rabbit. He was:

J. joyful **P.** playful   **B** beautiful **U** unique **N** nice **N** noticed **Y** young

Have children use the letters in their own names to describe how special they are too.

You're Special Too! Ask children to think about what makes James Philip Bunny special. What makes each of us different or special? They can write a story about their own special qualities. Ask children to keep a scrapbook showing their favorite things, their accomplishments, and their unique interests and qualities. They can also write about what makes each member of their family or class different or special.

RABBIT RESEARCHER

Rabbits are among the most common animals in the world. What kind of rabbit is J. P.? Help children decorate an old shoe box to make a rabbit hutch. Read about different kinds of rabbits, from cottontails to hares. What do rabbits eat? Find out about their habitats. For each fact you find, write it down and add it to the hutch.

COUNTING BUNNY HEADS

Materials:

tongue depressors or popsicle sticks   cotton balls or pom-poms
Q-tips or felt scraps   glue

Glue pom-poms or cotton balls to a popsicle stick for a bunny tail and add two pieces of felt or broken Q-tips for ears. Make as many as you want. Have children use the bunnies to practice counting. Count by ones using the whole bunny or each bunny tail. Count by twos using each pair of bunny ears. Count by threes using bunny ears and tails. Children can also turn their bunny sticks into hands-on counters to practice addition and subtraction.

About the author

Jacqueline Sweeney has published children's poems and stories in many anthologies and magazines. An author for Writers in the Schools and for Alternative Literary Programs in Schools, she has written numerous professional books on creative methods for teaching writing. She lives in Stone Ridge, New York.

About the photo illustrations

The photo illustrations are the collaborative effort of photographers G. K. and Vikki Hart and Blind Mice Studio. Following Mark Empey's sketched story board, G. K. and Vikki Hart photograph each animal and element individually. The images are then scanned and manipulated, pixel by pixel, by Mark and Kendra Empey at Blind Mice Studio.

Each charming illustration may contain from 15 to 30 individual photographs.

All the animals that appear in this book were handled with love. The ladybugs and butterflies were set free in the garden, while the others have been returned to or adopted by loving homes.